LORENZO'S MAGICAL LETTER

Carole York

Copyright 2021 Carole York

This book is dedicated to all the abused ponies in Ireland, abandoned by both their owners and their government

CHAPTER ONE

The goats came very late on Krismis Eve and they were trouble from the get go.
They were babies and their names were Liam and Lola and their horns were very small. I'd never seen goats before.

The lady got them collars with their names on in case they gapped it over the ditch into next door's. That was when she still liked them.

Liam, the boy goat, was grey and he had black legs and a black stripe all the way down his back. He walked in a wibbly wobbly way, nodding his head from side to side and wagging his fluffy little tail.

The girl goat was called Lola and she was brown. She also had a black stripe down her back but her legs weren't black, they were fawn. They had yellow eyes with a black stripe across the middle and they could roll them all the way around in their heads. I tried it once but it just made me dizzy and I fell over into a nettle patch.

MacDonald ran away, screaming, when he saw them.

MacDonald is our black and white cob, he's also got one blue eye like me. The Lady got him when he was a week old.

MacDonald had no mummy to teach him how to be a pony and we thought he was a bit dim.

The goats said they'd been waiting in Dublin all day

for Santy to bring them, they'd bought first class tickets to sit in the front of the sleigh but Santy was late because when he got as far as Belfast the reindeer said they needed a feed and they'd strike if they didn't get it and while we're at it we want a pay rise.

Reindeer be like bus drivers and pilots they always go on strike to cause the most inconvenience to the most number of people. Like when people want to go to work or go on their holliers. Krismis Eve was a good time to go on strike for reindeer and I made a note in my book to ask Pamela Anderson when might be a good time for ponies to go on strike.

The journey in the sleigh was very bumpy, the goats said, and Santy wouldn't let them sit in the front even though they'd paid for the first class tickets. They had to sit right in the back with the Krismis presents and they were so cross they ate a doll and a bicycle wheel and five boxes of After Eight mints and then they got sick over the rest of the presents. Lucky Santy didn't see it till he landed here or he would surely have thrown them out over

Waterford City and into the river.

Then Santy had to push them down the chimbly and Lola got stuck halfway and Liam behind her and Santy had to give them a shove with his big black boot. They were very cross when they landed in the grate, lucky the Lady didn't have the fire lit or they'd have been even crosser.

The Lady put them in with the chickens, we only had two left by then because the fox had come and eaten the rest of them and bit another one under her wing so the Lady put her in the kitchen to get better. The Lady is not a violent person but she got very violent that night cursing foxes. She said she was going to kill them and make Davy Crockett hats out of them.

"What's a Davy Crockett hat?" asked MacDonald, but nobody answered him because nobody knew what it was. I made a note in my book to ask the Lady what a Davy Crockett cap was at our next meeting.

CHAPTER TWO

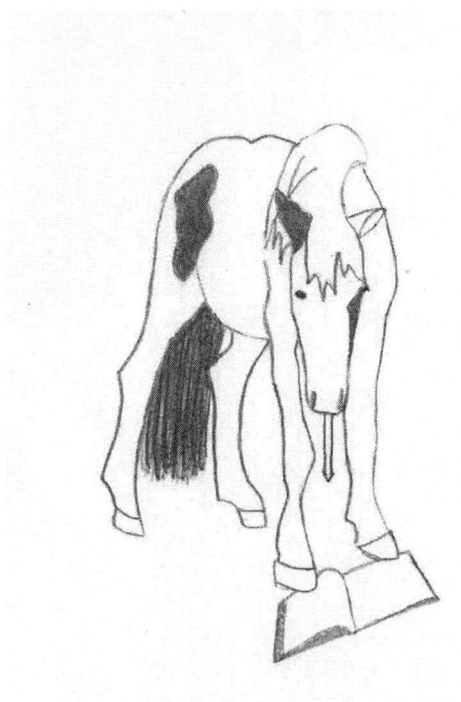

The other ponies thought I was weird when I first came

here because I have a blue eye and I don't talk alot. And I like to count things.

I count everything. I know how many trees there are in the paddock and how many buckets the Lady has to give us our feed and how many fence posts there are. I soon knew exactly how many times a day those goats went into places they weren't supposed to go.

I ran away a few times in the beginning but then the Lady gave me a job to do. She gave me a small notebook and a pencil.

"Matchbox," she said. " I want you to write down

everything that happens here and we'll have a meeting once a month so you can report on everything you've seen."
It's a very important job.
After three days the goats had eaten everything in the chicken pen except the 2 chickens. They ate all the ivy off the walls and then they started eating the chicken house so the lady put them in the garden amongst the trees and soon they had them ate too. There was nothing those goats didn't eat except the very thing they were supposed to eat, the ragwort.

Ragwort is poisonous to ponies and it grows all over the place in summer and that's why the Lady got the goats but she needn't have bothered because we don't like the taste of ragwort anyway so we don't eat it, not even Macdonald who didn't have a mummy to teach him. He just knew not to eat it.

The goats had only been here a week when the Lady left the conservatory door open and in they came. They were very nosey goats. The Small Pound Dog nearly lost her life when she saw them and she got the boy one by the front leg and shook it and then Dog ran up and caught him by the back leg and the Lady had to separate them all and she got bitten by the Small Pound Dog and pucked by the boy goat so she sent the Small Pound dog and Dog to jail for three days on bread and water. She would have sent the goats to jail too, but there were no cells left, them being full of dogs and Pamela Anderson who had broken into the feed room and eaten all the dog food.

The boy goat got a big bandage on his leg and it swelled up like a tennis ball and he hopped on 3 legs for a whole week.

The Lady was very, very cross and my notebook was getting very full.

I should splain that we've got three dogs here, one of them's been here since she was a pup straying on the Cork road, her name is Dog and she's a savage. The other two came from the pound in Carlow, one of them is a lurcher and the other one is a terror. Their names are Big Pound Dog and Small Pound Dog.

The goats were very posh, they said they came from Foxrock, where people talk in a funny accent nobody can understand except other people from Foxrock.

"Didn't you say you came from Kildare?" said Diablo.

Diablo is a Welsh pony. He's chestnut and he's a nutcase. The Lady says all chestnuts are nutcases.

"That was after we were in Foxrock," Liam replied.

"They lyin," said Frances, " nobody in Foxrock got goats. They only got mongrel dogs wid posh made up names like labradoodle and cavichon."

Frances is a black pony, she's very old and very grumpy. The dentist says she's 42 years old which is like 126 years old in people years so she's even older than the Lady. We don't argue with Frances because she can put a spell on you and your bottom goes on fire, just like that.

In February the real trouble started.

One night, the goats went to sleep on top of the bales stacked next to the shed which is next to the house. Goats can climb up on anything.

The Lady was sitting inside watching telly when she heard rats banging in the attic. At least that's what she thought it was.

"Dog," she said. "Get up in that attic and get rid of those rats."

"No way," said Dog. "Sounds more like elephants than rats. I'm not going up there. More than me life's worth."

"If you'd been doing your job in the first place instead of lying around on your bottom in front of the fire all winter there wouldn't be any rats ," replied the Lady and she put Dog under her arm and took her up the steps to the attic and shut the trapdoor and told her she wasn't coming out till all the rats were gone.

Dog ran around sniffing and scratching but she couldn't find any rats. She made more noise than the rats.

"No rats up here. Let me out," she shouted after half an hour.

The Lady let her out but the banging went on.

And that's when Pamela Anderson went to tell the Lady what we'd seen.

"Them goats is on the roof," she said.

"What?"

"On the roof an fightin on the chimbley stack."

"No way," said the Lady.

"Yes way," replied Pamela Anderson."They jumped off

the top of the bales and onto the shed roof and then they jumped onto the garage roof and then they...."

"Why are you only telling me this now?" the Lady interrupted her.

Interrupting someone when they're talking is very rude, that's what Pamela Anderson taught us but the Lady didn't care.

She ran out of the front door in her pajamas. They were new pajamas with Santys and reindeer on them, the Lady's mummy gave her them for Christmas.

The goats were galloping along the ridge from

chimbley to chimbley, weve got two chimblys, I don't know why, because we've only got one fireplace and I said how they manage to gallop like that?I'd be fallen off by now and Diablo said well how would you even get up there in the first place, you fool? I hadn't thought of that.

"What the hell are you doing up there?Get down !" the Lady roared. She didn't actually say hell, she said another word but it's on the forbidden list on account this is a children's book so I cant say it here. The goats only laughed at her and the boy one got up and stood on top of the chimbley. "We are lookout goats," he said. "We are watching for burglars."

It was half an hour before they came down and I had a crick in my neck watching them by then and Frances said she had a pain somewhere else I can't say here because it also on the forbidden list.

"You owe us a fiver," said the boy goat to the lady, once he'd jumped down. He jumped clean off the gable end and I thought for sure he'd break his neck but he just bounced on his little black legs and rolled his eyes around in his head.

"What?"

"A fiver. For lookout duties."

The lady told them to go away and chased them with a broom and they ran away and hid in the shed. Goats don't really run. They skip and they wobble and they do somersaults in the air.

The next day they went on the roof again, they ate the moss and cleaned out the gutters and did a very good job of it and they wanted a tenner each but the lady beat them down to a fiver between them.

CHAPTER THREE

Gordon would have been thrilled if he'd been around when the goats came. He could have retired Cat and gone goatjumping instead. The goats could jump seven feet easily, we knew this because the lady spent a whole morning building a paddock for them and they were only in it five minutes before they jumped out of it. Gordon was a mouse that used to live here. He only had one eye and he trained our one eyed cat to showjump and he went around wearing Superman knickers. He even held his own gymkhana and mice came from all over Ireland to compete in it.

But Gordon had blown himself up trying to launch a space shuttle he had made, off the roof of the house.

All that was left of him were his superman knickers that we found hanging off the lady's satellite dish. I had to give up my dream of becoming an astronaut when Gordon died because nobody else knew how to build a space shuttle, not even

Pamela Anderson, who is a very clever pony.

Gordon was a silly mouse but we loved him and we were all very sad when he died so we asked the lady to hang the knickers in the tree beside the little old dog's grave in the orchard so we could visit what was left of him whenever we liked. We had a funeral for the knickers anyway.

Diablo thought it would be a good idea to invite all the mice that had come down for the gymkhana and hundreds of them came, it was a very big funeral, but the problem was some of them wouldn't leave afterwards and a year later they were still here and some of them had babies.

"We in big trouble now," said Mario. "I told you it was a bad idea to invite all them mice, we should just have had a small funeral for friends and family an donations to the Disabled Mouse Foundation in lieu of flowers."

"What the Disabled Mouse Foundation?" said MacDonald. But nobody took any notice of him.

There were mice everywhere. The ones from Kerry were the worst, they'd bite you as soon as look at you. They got into the feed room and ate all our feed and what they didn't eat they poo'd on. We were all soon sick of spitting mouse poo out of our teeth.

And then the Goats stepped up.

"We are qualified Mouse Cursers," they said. "If you pay us a tenner we'll get rid of them."

I don't know what they did except there was alot of goat singing which nearly sent the Lady into a home for the bewildered but those mice were gone within the week. There was a situation later in the year when the goats got into an argument with the Lady and threatened to uncurse them but that's a story for another day.

CHAPTER FOUR

Then the big snow came. They

called it the Beast from the East and it snowed for five days solid, three feet deep and the Lady couldn't get the car up the driveway, which was just as well because she would have killed herself on the road for sure. The Lady didn't get worried until the electricity people said there'd be no major outages because whenever the electricity people say there'll be no outages you can be sure the lekkie going down the next day, the entire country.

It snowed and snowed and Frances stood out in it and

got covered all over her back. The next morning she looked like a snowman but that was ok because it's a good thing when the snow doesn't melt off your back it shows you're not losing your body heat. She could have gone in the garage if she wanted to, the lady even hung a haynet there but she didn't want to. Frances is a very contrary pony.

Then we ran out of hay and had to eat beetpulp till the weather cleared and the Lady could go and get more.

Pamela Anderson didn't get beetpulp and she complained to the lady but the lady said she wasn't interested because even thought there was no grass left and no hay to be had and Pamela Anderson ran around the track five times a day she was still the size of a barn side.

"It's not my fault" said Pamela Anderson. "I'm genetically modified."
I didn't know what that meant.

"If you say so." replied the lady
"So am I gettin feed tomorrow?"
"Nope"

"I'm reportin you to the Department," said Pamela Anderson
"Whatever you think yourself, pet," replied the Lady.
Pamela Anderson was always reporting the Lady to the Department of Agriculture but they never came.
The goats were freezing and shivering and the Lady felt sorry for them because they don't have woolly coats like ponies so she put them in the toolshed where they poo'd and pee'd all night so she didn't feel sorry for them again.
The ESB went down but luckily the Lady had cooked

a big pot of lentil stew. After three days she said she was never eating lentils again and gave it to the dogs but only the Big Pound Dog ate them. She ate anything because she'd been starving for years before the Lady took her in so she wasn't fussy, she said you never knew where your next meal was coming from. She told us she'd lived outside MacDonalds in Kilkenny for all her life, waiting for kind people to give her something. I cried when she told me that story but I didn't let anyone see me because they might laugh at me and call me a cissy.

On the second day of the Big Snow, Diablo and Pamela Anderson and Macdonald and Bon Bon went over the ditch into next door's .They hid there for five days until next door's came to complain they were frightening the cattle.Bon Bon said next door's had some cheek and his cattle coming over the ditch to our side all summer. So the lady had to put on her wellies and her wet gear and climb over the ditch to bring them back. She tripped and fell on the top of the ditch and I can't say here what she said.

"Would you like us to help you?" said the boy goat. "We are qualified pony catchers."

Them goats must have spent years in college to get all the qualifications they had. I made a note in my notebook to ask the Lady if I could go to college one day and learn to be a companion pony.

The Lady said no thankyou but the goats went with her anyway, nodding their goat heads from side to side and doing somersaults in the snow until the girl goat fell into a hole and had to be pulled out by the Lady.

It took the Lady half an

hour to find those ponies, the snow was so deep.

Diablo and Pamela Anderson said they weren't coming back so the Lady said they could stay there for the rest of their lives for all she cared, she was sick of them, but when they saw the goats making a run at them they changed their minds.

Everyone ran back over the ditch with the goats behind them and MacDonald knocked the Lady down and she lost her glasses, he was in such a hurry to get away from them. It was great craic altogether.

The Lady was in very bad

humour by the time she fixed the fence and got back to the house, her wellies full of snow.

The goats were waiting for her.

"That be a fiver. Each." said Liam.

"What?"

"Bringing ponies back. Should be a tenner with danger money but we giving you a discount on account of the snow in your wellies"

Once the snow melted Pete the Hayman came to us with his big trailer. The hayman is very nice, he comes straight away and puts the big round bales exactly where the Lady tells him to because she's too old to move them herself. They weigh 250kg.

In April, the Hayman ran out of hay, which had never happened before, so we were back on the beetpulp. The Lady put a post on her Facebook page asking could anyone bring us some hay and the very next day a big truck pulled up at the gate with 2 round bales.

A man we'd never seen before hopped over the gate. He'd brought hay all the way from Dungarvan for us. He said his name was John.

The Lady didn't know what to

say which isn't something
you see often because the
lady is always full of words.

CHAPTER FIVE

In the spring we got very exciting news about Tir na nOg who was the first pony that found his forever home. That was before my time but he was famous now. He was as mad as a boxful of frogs when he came here but then he got adopted and by now he'd taught three children to ride and had just got his fourth.
The Lady showed us pictures

of him all groomed and shiny and his mane plaited and shoes on his feet and right then I decided I wanted to be like him. I wrote to him and he sent me a picture wearing his fancy dress with his autograph on it and I stuck it in the back of my notebook with my picture of the Ninja shetland pony that the lady had given me after she died.

Diablo said I'd have to get over myself if I wanted to be like Tir na nOg.

"You're crazy, you wont even let the lady touch you let alone put a halter on you. What you gonna do when they want you to wear a saddle and bridle and put shoes on your feet? The last time the farrier came you jumped on his chest and he nearly didn't come back again."

I hadn't thought of that, but I thought I'd try anyway. I'd do it in memory of Gordon who had been my first friend at Putting in the Magic.

So I went to the lady and asked her what I had to do to become like Tir na nOg

"Well, first you'll have to let me put a headcollar on you"

"On my head?"

"Yes, that's usually where

the headcollar goes."

I said I'd think about it and I went to talk to Bon Bon, who'd been just like me when she arrived.

She told me that in the beginning something went pop in her head whenever she saw a headcollar.

"I couldn't help it," she said. "Something exploded in my head and it made my legs run. After a while it was less of a pop and more of a pinch and then I let them put the headcollar on me and it wasn't so bad."

"But how long did it take?"

"About two years."

"What? two years? I'll be

too old to be a showjumping pony by then."

"Yep. And another two years before I could stand the bridle on my head."

She wasn't very helpful and I thought I may as well give up on being like Tir na nOg and go back to being the Lady's secretary.

I was the only pony who could read and write apart from Pamela Anderson who can do everything.

But I still wanted to make something more of myself.

CHAPTER SIX

In the summer, the goats started riding Mario. They waited till he was eating his dinner and then they jumped up on the dog kennel and onto his back. Mario got very cross and complained to the Lady but she said she couldn't do anything about it so Dog offered to bite them and the Lady locked her up. Dog is a vermin.

They said they were getting fit for their trip to South Africa and jumping on and off Mario was like going to the gym.

"What trip to South Africa?" said Diablo..

"We are going to South Africa on our holidays. We going Great White Shark Cage Diving in Cape Town."

"What Shark Cage divin?" asked MacDonald

"You get in a cage and they

Lower you into the sea and the sharks come to look at you," said the goats.

"And you drown. That if the sharks dont eat you first. I hear sharks be partial to a bit of tasty Irish goat." said Diablo

"We won't drown. We are expert swimmers, weve swum at the Goat Olympics."

Pamela Anderson hit them then, she said she'd never heard such liars in her life. They were worse than Frances. Then Snip saw an advert for a job at a stud farm and he applied. Snip was a big bay pony but he had a sore back and he couldn't be ridden so

nobody wanted to adopt him.
Frances couldn't stop laughing.

"Who goin give you a job at a stud farm, you clown? Do you even know what they do at stud farms? You a gelding. You won't be able. Ha. Ha ha ha. Ha ha ha."

I remember Snip made himself very big and sniffed at her.

"You don't know anything. It's a job to be a grandaddy to baby foals when they leave their mummies," he said, and he bit her on the bottom, which made her stop laughing straight away.

Anyway, Snip got the job and they came to collect him the

next day and he went off to Kilkenny and never even looked back at us and three months later the stud farm people sent the lady a letter and some money saying they were very happy with his work.

I started looking in the paper for pony jobs, I thought perhaps I could make some use of myself as a foal grandaddy like Snip but there weren't any jobs advertised, only jobs for showjumpers and lead rein ponies and dressage ponies and companion ponies.

"All them jobs you have to wear a headcollar, there's

no way around it," said Bon Bon

"Even companion ponies?"

"Yep"

I didn't believe her so I went to ask the Lady why I had to wear a headcollar if I was only going to run around in a field being a friend to another pony.

" Well, for starters how am I going to get you into the horsebox?"

"What horsebox?"

"The one you'll have to travel in to your new home."

"No. I'm not going in a horsebox again."

The Lady just shook her head and walked away.

One weekend some of the Lady's friends came and they flogged themselves to death to put up fencing along the ditch but that night after the Lady had gone to bed MacDonald walked through the fence and gapped it into next door's and Diablo and Pamela Anderson followed him.

The Lady went at the crack of dawn and got them back following a bucket because they were running around all over the place and wouldn't come back.
Then, after the Lady fixed the fence and went inside

for a cup of tea MacDonald got up on top of the ditch and walked all along looking for another place to break out.

Mario ran to tell the Lady "He's at it again, he's on top of the ditch he said and the Lady shouted and poked him with a stick until he came down. After that he went to jail for the entire day and the Lady accidentally hit herself on the head with the pick axe handle and gave herself a black eye. She was in bad form for the rest of the day.

When summer came and the

ragwort started growing the Lady told the goats to eat it but they wouldn't. They slept on the Lady's garden chairs most of the day and the rest of the time they spent stripping bark off the Lady's apple trees. One day they ate 12 docks, one rose bush, the Small Pound Dog's breakfast, one Tesco shopping bag, Mario's dinner, a small patch of ivy, and a fieldmouse. In all the time they were here, before the Lady sent them back to where they came from, I never saw them eat a single ragwort. They were idle blackguards.

CHAPTER SEVEN

Halfway through the summer we got a new pony.
His name was Buster but the Lady didn't like that name so she changed it to Christopher Robin.

He was the most handsome pony I had ever seen. He was pure white with a long mane and tail and soft brown eyes. I wished I looked like him. Maybe if I looked like him somebody would want to adopt me.

But I didn't look anything like him. I had short legs and brown patches and one of my eyes was blue. Maybe it was the blue eye that put people off me but there was no way of changing that. I was trying so hard to let the lady put the headcollar on me but the thing in my head was till going pop and I couldn't.

The lady put him in a paddock on his own like she always does with a new pony, in case there's mucksavagery. Pamela Anderson is always the first to check out the new ponies but she was away on her holliers so we didn't know what to do.

MacDonald started walking down the track and Diablo said where do you think you're going and he said to say hello to the new pony.

"No you're not, nobody can say hello to new ponies until Pamela Anderson sees them."

"She not here, she on her holliers, nobody goin to

talk to him for 6 weeks?"
Then Frances spoke.
" I know that pony," she said.
"Don't lie,"said Diablo, "that pony's from Cork and you were never in your life in Cork."
"Well, he was in Louth before he was in Cork. He had a eye operation.When they saved me from the pound they put me in a stable next to him. After, they put us in the same field and then someone adopted him and took him to Cork but nobody wanted me because I was old and I wouldn't have the headcollar. I haven't seen

him for six years."

She ran down the track to where he was. They touched noses over the fence and I ran to call the Lady.

"Frances and the new pony touching noses over the fence," I shouted, so the Lady put her in with him and they spent ages sniffing each other and touching noses. I think the Lady cried when she saw it, because Frances had no friends until then.

The Lady cries for everything, its hard to tell if she's happy or sad.

CHAPTER EIGHT

In June Mario started standing at the gate every day.
"What's he at?" said Diablo.
"I dunno, he's waiting for the Postman, must be expecting a parcel," said MacDonald.
And then a campervan arrived and out of it stepped a very small yellow pony with a stripe down her back. We thought she was a goat and

we couldn't understand a word she she said.

She came with two rugs and her own feed bucket and an electric fence, not that that mattered because she never stayed inside it no matter what the Lady did, she went wherever she pleased.

She said her name was Cindy and she was from Cobh. We didnt' know where Cobh was and she said it was in China and we believed her, the little liar.

"What she sayin?" asked MacDonald.

"Dunno, must be Chinese she talkin," replied Christopher

Robin.

Mario went mad when he saw her.

"Welcome. Welcome my bride!" he shouted.

"What bride?" said Diablo.

"Yeah, what bride?" said MacDonald

He told us he'd been on the internet and ordered a wife from Mail order Brides in China. He was so proud.

"That pony not from China," said Frances, " I seen Chinese ponies an they don't look like that.That pony's from Cobh."

"Cobh is in China," said Mario

"Who told you that? Cobh is

in Cork you numpty."

"No it's not, they say on the website it's in China"

"They can say whatever they like on a website but I'm telling you Cobh is in Cork," said Frances

But Mario wasn't having any of it so Diablo said leave him off, who cares where she's from. One thing for sure she looks like trouble. And he was right.

Cindy was a maniac, she went around kicking everybody and I decided I definitely didn't want to be like her. She growled at Diablo across the fence and jumped up on her hind legs and stamped her front feet. First time I ever heard a pony growl, the Lady said it was because she had lived her whole life with dogs and she didn't know how to behave around other ponies. She even went in the house like a dog.

She ran up and showed her bottom to Frances. Then she ran down to Bon Bon and kicked her with both back feet, then she hunted Mario all round the track and after that she kicked Christopher Robin in his knee with her front foot.

We didn't know what to do so we decided to stay well away from her. The Lady had to get

Pamela Anderson back from her holliers to put manners on her.

Cindy didn't have a long mane like us, she had a brush cut and a week after she arrived the goats tried to hire her out to the Lady as a chimbly sweep for a tenner, they said they'd shove her up the chimney and catch her when she came out the top.

"No pony going up a chimney, here," said the Lady. "What about Health and Safety?"

"She's experienced. She's got a ticket. She's been doing it all over Cobh for years and she's famous," the goats replied.

"Did she tell you that?" said the Lady.

"Not exactly," replied the goats.

"So what exactly did she say?"

"She said she's been in the Paddy's Day Parade in Cobh for three years."

The Lady said being in the Paddy's Day Parade did not qualify you to clean chimbleys although she did say she'd once seen a fella try to climb up the pub chimbley on Paddy's Day after he'd drunk sixteen pints of Guinness.

"Cindy says she'll give it a

lash for a tenner," said Liam.

"I'm warning you, " said the Lady. "If you try to push that pony up the chimney there will be severe consequences."

But the goats didn't care and when the Lady came back from town they had Cindy stuck halfway up the chimbley and couldn't shift her up or down and the Lady had to call the Fire Brigade to get her out.

CHAPTER NINE

Cindy didn't like Mario and when we told her she had to like him because he paid for her to be his wife she said she didn't care, she wasn't going to be his wife and end of. Pamela Anderson boxed her ears but it made no difference. Cindy was a very stubborn pony.
Mario was very upset, and we felt very sorry for him. He asked me to write a letter to the Mail Order Bride

people for him.

Dear Mail Order Brides

I am returning the bride you sold me. She's not fit for purpose. First she ran off with Pamela Anderson and then yesterday she kicked the bottom off me twice.

I saved all my wages the lady paid me for being the watch pony to pay for her.

I even had a bath and clip but she still ran off.

In case you don't know, the watch pony is the one tells the lady when someone's at the gate and if ponies gap it over the ditch into next doors. It's a very hard job and minimum wage and I saved

for 6 months.
I am sending her back by train you can pick her up in Cobh tomorrow and please send my money back.
Yours faithfully
Super Mario (that's my full name be used in all crosspondence)
But they wouldn't take her back so we were stuck with her. At least the Lady felt sorry for him and she gave him a wage increase.
It was the hottest summer ever, after the worst winter ever and as soon as the grass started growing it stopped raining and everything got burnt. The

Lady had to start feeding us hay in July.
When the round bales came Cindy pulled out the middles and got inside and the Lady couldn't find her for a week. The heat must have fried the Lady's brain because she let MacDonald into the kitchen and nearly had a disaster, she forgot he was a yearling the last time he was in the kitchen and now he was a 2 years old and twice the size and he got stuck between the kitchen table and the frigerator. The Lady said it was like turning the Queen Mary around in a swimming pool. I had to ask Pamela

Anderson who was Queen Mary and she said it was a big ship owned by the Queen of England and then I had to ask her who was the Queen of England and she smacked my ears I don't know why, so I still don't know who the Queen of England is and I'm not asking again

Cindy was a very clever pony, nearly as clever as Pamela Anderson.
She tied 2 buckets with baling twine and put them on so one hung each side of her back and went to see the Lady.
"What do you want?" said the

Lady.

"I'm applying for the job."

"What job?"

"Pamela Anderson says you looking for a Kitchen Pony."

"Am I? That's the first I've heard of it," replied the Lady.

"I can bake. I baked you 2 gluten free vegetarian pies. Look in the bucket."

"I only see one."

"I ate the other one.

"What's in the other bucket?"

"A lettuce and 6 carrots. I grew them myself."

"I only see a lettuce."

"I don't eat lettuce," said Cindy.

The Lady gave her the job but she didn't last long because she went in the feed room and ate all the dog food so she got the sack.

CHAPTER TEN

Then the goats saw a pony in trouble in Limerick on the internet and decided to adopt it for a fiver.

They wanted to go with the Lady to Limerick to collect him but she said not in this Lifetime am I driving two goats to Limerick.

The goats were waiting for her when she got back.

"Did you get our pony?"

"I did."

"So where is he?" said Liam.

"He's in foster for a month with Miriam," the Lady replied.

"WHAT? WE BEEN BUSY ALL DAY GETTIN HIS STABLE READY! WE CLEANED OUT THAT HOVEL YOU MAKE US SLEEP IN AN PUT FRESH HAY AN ALL. WE GOIN SLEEPING ROUGH SO HE CAN BE INSIDE!" Liam shouted.

"Did you get his marking sheet off the vet?" asked Lola. "We've decided to name him Reginald Goatpony. Do you want me to spell it for you? For the passport, like?"

"Miriam has named him Fudge," the Lady replied and the goats started shouting again.

"What? NO! HIS NAME IS REGINALD GOATPONY! After our maternal grandfather, may he rest in peace in a bog in Leitrim. We are reporting you to the Department. An Mary Lou Macdonald."

The Lady said they could report her to the Department, they could report her to Mary Lou MacDonald, they could report her to Mary Poppins for all she cared and she went to bed.

"You hear that, Lola? Who the heck is Mary Lou MacDonald?" said Liam.

"Damned if I know. Might be MacDonald's sister?" replied Lola.

Reginald Goatpony was brown all over and his teeth didn't meet properly but it didn't bother him, he was well able to eat, he was as round as a ball.

When he came back from Miriam's, Pamela Anderson called a Pony Council Meeting so he could tell his story.

The goats led him down to the meeting place under the willow trees at the bottom of the paddock. He was very good to walk on the lead rope and I made a note to ask him how he learned to do that.

"No goats," said Pamela Anderson.

"Why not?" said Liam.

"Because this is a Pony Council meeting and you are not ponies."

"But he's our pony, we have to stay with him to make sure he's safe."

Pamela Anderson lowered her head very slowly and stared at him. Then she started twitching her bottom and we knew she was getting ready to turn around and kick him.

"Go," she said, and the goats went to hide on top of the hill where the briars grow, they thought we couldn't see them but we could and Diablo said he'd burst them after the meeting, for pulling faces and making rude signs and showing us their bottoms.

"So what happened to you?" said Pamela Anderson.

"I was tied to a lekkie gate at a buildin yard with blue rope around my neck" he said."Every time a lorry went in or out the gate I had to run up and down and my legs got tangled in the rope and made a hole and bugs got in and made a fection. After a while I was so tangled I couldn't walk any more.And then a Lady saw me and cut me loose."

"How old are you?" asked Mario.

"I'm ten years old in June," he said.

"The Lady told us you were 36 inches high but you're way bigger than that. You grow since you left Limerick?"

" No, I only said that because I was afraid the goats wouldn't take me if I was bigger. I'm 44 inches."

"Goats got nothing to do with it," snorted Pamela Anderson. You can be 48 inches and the Lady will still take you."

The dentist came on a day the sky was black and windy and the rain lashing down. The Lady had only enough money to pay for three ponies so Pamela Anderson drew tickets out of a feed bucket.

" I don't wanna be in the feed bucket," said Frances and she gave Pamela Anderson a fiver to keep her name out of it but Pamela Anderson took the fiver and put her in the bucket anyway.

The three ponies were Frances, Diablo and Bon Bon.

It took Lisa and the Lady half an hour to get a headcollar on Diablo. Mainly

Lisa, because the Lady said she was too old to be going in the stable with him to be kicked to death but Lisa's afraid of nothing. She's been helping the Lady for years and she knows everything about ponies, she's nearly as clever as Pamela Anderson. Frances was livid and called Pamela Anderson alot of rude names and threatened to set her bottom on fire at the next New Moon.

The dentist found a rotten tooth and pulled it out. It stank to high heaven and Frances was so happy after, that she changed her mind about setting Pamela

Anderson's bottom on fire. She said she'd had a toothache for years.

That's why she was so grumpy, I'd be grumpy if I'd had toothache for years.

CHAPTER ELEVEN

Lorenzo came in October. He was black and white and he was a mergency.
He was so small they brought him in the middle of the night in the back of a jeep. We didn't spot him till the next morning. He was very

thin because the bad people had not been feeding him and they'd been sitting on his back and making him pull a cart with five big lads in it. They'd nailed shoes on his back feet and the Lady nearly had a fit when she saw them.

His back was very sore and his back leg was wonky and he had a cough and his eyes were infected. He was a very sorry looking animal. Pamela Anderson looked in his mouth and said he was only three months old.

He said he was a girl and he was a Special Agent for the PIA and he was on a secret mission. We found out much later that he wasn't a girl at all, he was a boy, and he wasn't a Special Agent for the PIA either. He made it all up because he was frightened the bad people would come looking for him and take him away.

He didn't even have a name when he came and it was a few days before a big storm called Storm Lorenzo hit us and the Lady called him Lorenzo.

That was a good name for him because he became a very troublesome pony and caused more bother than ten storms.

The Lady put Pamela Anderson

in the stable with him to mind him, Pamela Anderson always minds the new ponies and the next day Lisa came and took the nasty shoes off him and the Lady let them out into the front garden.

We didn't see much of him to begin with because the Lady kept him mostly in the kitchen except at night when he slept on the front doorstep. It was November by then and getting cold so Cindy lent him her best rug. In January the landlord sent us a letter saying he was going to sell our home and throw us all out and the Lady too and we'd be homeless. We asked him to to give us time to save up the money to buy it ourselves but he wouldn't.

Lorenzo raffled his shoes and got €200 and gave it all to the Lady except a fiver he kept for himself in case he needed taxi fare to go to town.

Then he decided to write a letter to God and tell him we were in serious bother and could he please help us. Since he couldn't write himself, he asked me to write it for him and not to tell anyone about it, in case everyone thought he was mad.

I told him I didn't know if writing to God was such a good thing because you never knew what he might do, him being God and all. But he nagged me for so long that I changed my mind. We didn't hear back from God for a while, I suppose he must have been quite busy, he must have a heap of Personal Assistants checking his mail. But when we did hear back we got a very big answer.

In February, just before we were supposed to be homeless the goviment said everyone had to stay at home and the landlord wasn't allowed to throw us out because there was a big virus, worse than the one Lorenzo got in his eye and chest. At first we thought it was a good thing and Lorenzo asked me to write another letter to God to thank him for helping us but soon all the hospitals were full and people were getting very sick and dying and we got a fright then.

"Best you keep quiet about that letter in case we get into trouble and you get sent back to the bad people," I said.

" It's not my fault. I never asked God to do all that," he replied. "I think he overreacted."

"I know. But that's what happens when you ask God for help. You never know what way he's going to help you."

Lorenzo stared at me for a bit and then he folded the letter up very small and hid it in the coal bunker when nobody was looking.

The landlord left us in peace for two years but now he's at it again. We daren't write another letter to God after what happened the last time.

We've been saving all our money and last summer Lorenzo made vegetarian pies and sold them at our gate and I got myself a flock of rescue hens and I sold their eggs. Alot of people have given us money but it's still not enough so we'll have to keep going. Perhaps a kind person will see the trouble we're in and buy our home for us so we can stay here forever and get more ponies away from the bad people.

That would be the best Krismis present ever.

                 THE END